Flash Flood

by

Andy Croft

Illustrated by Aleksandar Sotirovski

For Holly and Babette

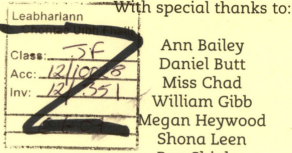

With special thanks to:

Ann Bailey
Daniel Butt
Miss Chad
William Gibb
Megan Heywood
Shona Leen
Ben Shipley
Spencer
Sophie Strawbridge

First published in 2009 in Great Britain by
Barrington Stoke Ltd
18 Walker St, Edinburgh, EH3 7LP

www.barringtonstoke.co.uk

ISBN: 978-1-84299-607-2

Printed in Great Britain by Bell & Bain Ltd

Contents

Chapter 1
Rain, Rain, Go Away

It was still pouring with rain. Jaz gazed out of the caravan window. There were huge puddles all over the field. One of the caravans was standing in a small lake. It seemed as if it had been raining for ever. Someone said it was the wettest summer for years.

Jaz and Toni had been best mates since they started Brownies. They did everything together. They liked the same music. The same soaps. They even fancied the same boys.

But after a week in this caravan they were getting on each other's nerves. And all because of the rain. There was a tennis court on the site. But it was under water.

There was a table-tennis table in the Games Room. But Toni thought table-tennis was boring. They played cards. But Toni said it was boring. They played on Jaz's DS. They read mags. They went for walks in the rain. But Toni was always bored.

Of course there wasn't a telly. Every night they played Scrabble. Toni's dad won; as he always did. He thought he was clever, playing words like RAIN, WET and FLOOD.

"Very funny," said Toni. When it was her turn she spelled the word BORED.

Jaz gave a sigh. If only it would stop raining. She looked out of the window again. Toni was running across the field. The wash-room was the other side of the camp-site. They got soaked every time they went to the toilet.

Toni slammed the caravan door behind her. "I'm soaked!" she said as she kicked off her wellies. "I've had enough. I want to go home!"

"You know we're going home tomorrow," said her mum.

"Well, I want to go home now. I'm bored of this rain."

Toni's dad put down his newspaper. "Why don't you and Jaz go swimming? We can give you a lift into town when we go shopping."

Toni snorted. "We don't need to go to the baths. There's plenty of water outside. We'll soon have to swim to the toilet!"

Toni's mum looked up from her book. "Look, we didn't make it rain. If you'd had a proper coat you wouldn't be so wet."

"But I'd still be bored!" Toni put her wellies back on. "Come on, Jaz."

Jaz grabbed her coat and followed her outside. Toni slammed the caravan door behind them.

It was still raining.

Chapter 2
The Old House

The Games Room was full.

"Typical," said Toni. "Now what? Under water tennis?"

"Let's walk into town," said Jaz. "We can find a nice warm café. Maybe you can get a signal."

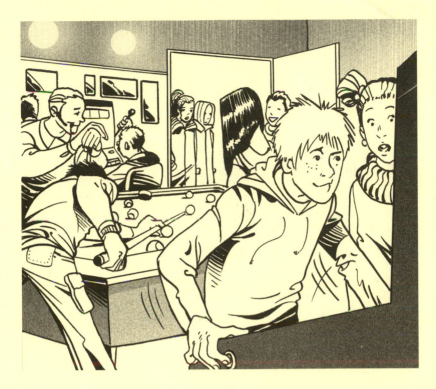

"But it's miles away!" said Toni.

"Not if we take the short-cut by the river."

They climbed the gate at the end of the field.

"Wow! Just look at all that water!" said Jaz.

The river was really full. It was flowing very fast. Whole trees raced by in the current. A family of ducks swam past.

"At least someone's enjoying all this rain," Toni grumbled. "I'm bored."

They walked in silence along the muddy river bank. Jaz gave a sigh. If only Toni would stop moaning.

Suddenly the sky grew dark. There was a rumble of thunder. Jaz and Toni both screamed.

"I'm scared!" shouted Toni. "Let's go back."

They turned round. But the path was now under water. They were cut off.

"I don't understand," said Toni.

"The river must have broken its banks," said Jaz.

There was another crash of thunder. This time it seemed very close. The girls screamed again. It started pouring down.

"What are we going to do?" shouted Toni.

"What?" shouted Jaz. She couldn't hear Toni above the noise of the rain.

"What are we going to do?"

"Well, we can't go back," said Jaz.

"What?"

"We can't go back. We've got to find some shelter."

"What?"

Jaz pointed through the rain.

"Look! I think there's a house over there. Come on!"

The girls splashed along the river bank through the water and the rain to the house. The rain was cold and hard on their frozen faces. Their hands were numb. Their feet were soaking. Toni was crying.

Jaz banged on the door. "Please let us in!" she shouted. There was no answer. Only the sound of the thunder and the rain. Toni banged on the door again. "Help! We're wet and we're scared!"

Jaz tried the door handle. It swung open.

Inside it was cold and dark. The old house smelled of cob-webs and damp. No-one had lived there for years. There was an old kitchen table, a rusty bike and some plastic oil-drums. Someone had tried to use the chairs for firewood. The axe was still there.

Toni sat down on one of the chairs.

"Well, at least we're safe here," she said.

Then she froze.

In the middle of the table sat a big, brown rat.

Chapter 3
Trapped

Toni screamed. She ran up the stairs.

Jaz grabbed the axe and ran after her.

There were two rooms upstairs. In one

room there was an old cupboard. They

squeezed inside the cupboard and pulled the

door shut.

"I'm scared," said Jaz.

"Me too."

"I hate rats."

"Me too."

They stood there in the dark for ages. After a while Toni had an idea.

"I'll ring my dad," she whispered. "He'll come and rescue us." She flipped open her phone. No signal.

Jaz opened the cupboard door. Very slowly.

"Is it safe?" asked Toni.

Jaz nodded. There was no sign of the rat.

In the other room was a mattress. Someone had smashed all the glass out of the window. The damp curtains were flapping in the wind. Toni peered outside.

"Jaz – what's happened to the fields? They've gone!"

The fields were under water. So were some of the trees. The river was now a huge lake. The tops of the trees were like green islands in a silver sea.

"We're in trouble," said Jaz. "We've got to get out of here."

"What about the rat?" asked Toni.

"Never mind the rat," said Jaz. "Come on. If we don't get out of this house soon, we'll never –"

She stopped at the top of the stairs. Below them, the kitchen was now under water. The table was floating like a boat. The plastic drums were bobbing against the stairs.

Jaz and Toni were trapped.

Chapter 4
Don't Panic

The girls were sitting on the old mattress. They were both hungry and cold. Big drops of rain dripped through holes in the roof. And they were still thinking about the rat. Toni shivered.

"I'm freezing," said Toni.

"Me too."

"I'm starving."

"Me too."

"I wish we were back in that nice warm caravan."

"Me too."

"I can't believe I just said that."

"Me too."

Neither of them laughed.

Toni shivered again. "Jaz, what are we going to do?"

"We could light a fire," said Jaz.

"How? We haven't got any matches."

"Rub sticks together. I've seen it on telly."

"Stop joking," said Toni. "I'm scared."

She flipped open her mobile phone. Still no signal.

"Do you think Mum and Dad are OK? Suppose the caravan park is flooded?" She bit her lip. "Jaz, I want to go home. What if –"

"Don't worry," said Jaz, "I am sure they're safe. Your dad will come and rescue us, just you see."

"Well, how long are we going to be stuck here?"

"Until the water goes down. It must stop sometime."

"But what if it doesn't stop? What if this house is washed away? We can't stay here. And the water's far too cold for swimming."

Jaz stared down at the smelly brown water. It was now half way up the stairs.

"You're right. We need a boat."

"But we haven't got a boat!"

"I know. We're going to make one."

Chapter 5
All Aboard

"First we need some planks," said Jaz.

"Planks? Where are we going to find them?"

Jaz picked up the axe. She smashed the axe against the cupboard. The door fell off in one piece. "And some rope."

"Rope? What for?"

Jaz thought for a minute. "We could tear those curtains," she said. "They're a bit smelly. But they look strong."

Toni pulled the curtains down. Then she started tearing them into strips.

"Great," said Jaz. "Now get those plastic oil drums. Four of them should do the trick."

She picked up the axe and attacked the cupboard again.

Toni crept to the edge of the stairs. The flood had almost reached the top step. The plastic oil drums were floating in the dirty water. Toni stretched out her arm.

Got it.

Then another.

Then another.

She was going to grab the last one. Then she saw the rats. This time there were two of them. And they were swimming towards her. Toni screamed.

Jaz came running.

"What's the matter?"

"Give me the axe!" shouted Toni.

"Why?"

Toni grabbed the axe and threw it. The rats disappeared. The axe landed with a splash into the water.

"What are you doing?" shouted Jaz. "I was using that!"

"I'm sorry, Jaz. I didn't think. I was just –"

"Oh, never mind," said Jaz. "Hold my hand."

"What?"

"Just do it. And don't let go!"

Toni held Jaz's hand. The water had now reached the top of the stairs. Jaz stretched out over the cold, dark flood. Her fingers grabbed the handle on the plastic drum.

"Got it!"

They rolled the plastic drums together.

"Come on!" said Jaz. "We don't have much time!"

There was water all over the floor. They tied the drums together as fast as they could. But their cold fingers kept slipping on the wet curtains.

"Faster!" yelled Jaz.

By now the drums were beginning to float. Both girls were really scared.

"Faster!"

"I'm trying!"

They were now up to their knees in the smelly brown water. They tied the planks on top of the drums. In a few minutes the room would be flooded.

"Right, get the other end of the mattress."

They tried to lift it. But the wet
mattress was too heavy.

"I can't lift it!" shouted Toni. "It's no
use."

"Try harder!" screamed Jaz.

"I can't!"

The water was pouring into the room.

"Yes, you can!"

"I can't!"

"After three. One, two, three, NOW!"

With one last effort they lifted the mattress on top of the planks. They jumped onto the little raft. It was spinning round in circles. Jaz used a plank to keep it still.

The water had now reached the window sill.
Jaz pushed the plank against the wall. The
raft sailed towards the broken window.

"Duck!" shouted Jaz. They put their
heads down.

"Goodbye, rats!" shouted Toni.

And they sailed out of the house.

Chapter 6
Splash!

They were in a bright, cold world of light and water. The green fields were now a flat shiny mirror of grey. Everything seemed silent and still. They could see for miles.

"It's awesome!" said Toni.

"Amazing!" yelled Jaz.

At that moment the sun came out from behind a cloud.

"Look! It's stopped raining!"

The girls high-fived.

"This is fantastic!" cried Toni. "It's so quiet. Like we are the last people in the world."

They sailed on in silence for several minutes. Then Toni held out her hand to Jaz.

"I'm sorry about this week," she said. "Sorry I've been in such a bad mood."

"That's OK," said Jaz.

"No it's not. I've been rubbish to you. You see – I just wanted you to have a good time. I've been looking forward to this holiday for ages. I didn't want you to be bored. And if it wasn't for the stupid rain –"

"You're the stupid one," said Jaz. "The only thing that was boring was you. Always saying you were bored. Anyway –"

"Look out!" Toni shouted. They were floating towards a tree. Its long, spiky branches were drifting in the water. Jaz picked up the loose plank. But the wet wood slipped in her cold hands. She tried to catch it and lost her balance. She slipped over the side with a great SPLASH!

"Jaz!" yelled Toni.

Jaz swam to the surface, gasping for breath. Toni grabbed her arm. Jaz was blue with cold.

"Pull!"

"I'm trying!" Toni said.

"Well, try harder!"

"I'm trying harder!"

Very slowly, Toni pulled Jaz out of the water and onto the mattress. Her clothes were soaking wet. Her skin was icy cold.

"I'm f-f-freezing," she stammered.

"Take off your wet things," said Toni.
"You can wear my coat and jumper. I'm not
cold. It's quite warm in the sunshine."

Jaz did as she was told.

"Aye, aye captain," she said.

The river was now taking them down stream. The current pushed and pulled the little raft faster and faster. In a few minutes they reached the caravan site. They sailed past clothes and chairs and toys floating in the water. The ducks were still splashing about.

The caravans were drifting around in the flood like sinking ships. Toni's parents were sitting on the roof of their car. They looked very wet and cold. And a bit scared. The water was only a few inches away from their feet. And it was still rising.

Chapter 7
One Year Later

Toni and Jaz were sitting in the new caravan. They were playing Scrabble with Toni's parents.

After last year's flood, the old caravan was no good any more. They had sold it for scrap. The new one was cool. It was much bigger. It even had a telly. But these days Jaz and Toni were into Scrabble.

Toni's dad was winning, of course.

"There we are," said Toni's dad. He put his letters on the board. HEROES. Everyone laughed. That was what the local paper had called Jaz and Toni last summer – "TEENAGE HEROES."

They'd rowed Toni's mum and dad to safety. Then they'd gone back for other people trapped by the flood.

It seemed a long time ago now. A bit like a dream.

Toni looked down at the letters in front of her.

"I can't go."

Her dad looked over her shoulder. "Yes you can, love," he said. "You can spell your favourite word – BORING."

Toni grinned. "I'm not playing that. I'm never going to say I'm bored again. Anyway, I like being bored!"

Everyone grinned again. Toni's mum stood up to put the kettle on. Jaz looked out of the caravan window.

It was just starting to rain ...

Snow Dogs

by
Jane A. C. West

Zeb wants to win the dog sled race. But will he die before he gets to the end?

You can order *Snow Dogs* from our website at www.barringtonstoke.co.uk

Cliff Edge

by
Jane A. C. West

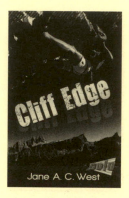

Can Danny make the climb of his
life to save his friend? No ropes,
no help – no hope?

You can order *Cliff Edge* from our website at
www.barringtonstoke.co.uk

United, Here I Come!

by
Alan Combes

Joey and Jimmy are very bad at football.
But Jimmy is sure he will play for United
one day. Is Jimmy crazy?

You can order *United, Here I Come!* from our website at
www.barringtonstoke.co.uk